W9-AHA-758

First edition for the United States and Canada published 1987 by
Barron's Educational Series

First published 1987 by Piccadilly Press Ltd.,
London, England.

Text and illustrations © Richard Fowler, 1987

All inquiries should be addressed to:
Barron's Educational Series, Inc.
250 Wireless Boulevard
Hauppauge, New York 11788

Library of Congress Catalogue Card No. 87-14003
International Standard Book No. 0-8120-5878-X

Library of Congress Cataloging-in-Publication Data
Fowler, Richard, 1944-
Cat's cake.

Summary: Cat's animal friends all like his cake,
but each wishes it was flavored with just a little
more of his own favorite thing.
1. Cake--Fiction.   2. Animals--Fiction.   I. Title.
PZ.F8296Cat   1987   [E] 87-14003
ISBN 0-8120-5878-X

Printed in Portugal by Printer Portuguesa
789 9697 987654321

Cat's Cake

Richard Fowler

BARRON'S
New York . Toronto

Cat baked a cake.
He was very pleased with it,
so he tried it out on the
bear next door.

"Yum, yum," grunted Bear.
"It's delicious, but . . .
another time perhaps a little
honey would help!"

"Oh well," sighed Cat.
"I'll see if Penguin would
like a piece."
  "Yum, yum," snapped Penguin.
"It's very good, but . . .
some fish would make
it even better!"

"Never mind," thought Cat.
"I'll see if Tiger would like a slice."
"Yum, yum," purred Tiger.
"Perfect cake, but . . .
I think a little meat would
improve the flavor!"

Cat offered Rabbit a slice of cake.

"Yum, yum," mumbled Rabbit.

"It's scrumptious, but . . ."

"Don't tell me," sighed Cat.

"It needs a few carrots added to it!"

"How did you guess?" laughed Rabbit.

Suddenly Monkey swung down out of
a tree and grabbed a piece of cake.
    "Bananas, bananas, that's what it
needs!" chuckled Monkey,
then jumped up into another tree.

As Cat walked home, he
went by the field where Goat lived.

"I hear you baked a cake," said Goat.
"Have you got a piece for me?"
Cat gave Goat the last slice.

"Yum, yum!" exclaimed Goat.
"It's super but . . .
there is not enough of it!"

"That's the nicest thing I've heard
all day," said Cat.

"Maybe I'll bake another cake
next week."

A week later Cat was back in the kitchen.

"Everyone likes chocolate cake!" said Cat
as he carefully weighed the ingredients:
eggs, flour, cocoa, chocolate,
butter, and sugar.

"Oh bother! There's not enough sugar.
I'll just run out to the store," said Cat.

While Cat was out, Bear came
along, sniffing the air.

"Good, I was right," said Bear.
"Cat is making another cake!"

He reached in through the kitchen window
and poured a jar of honey into the mixing bowl.

A moment later Penguin leaned
through the window and popped
a shiny fish into the cake mixture!

Then Tiger popped a big paw
through the window and dropped a pound
of fresh raw meat into the bowl.

"This should be a grrreat cake!"
growled Tiger.

Rabbit hopped up to the window, made sure
no one was looking, then pushed three
large carrots into the cake mixture.

"That will make it a crunchy chocolate cake!"
giggled Rabbit.

Monkey stuffed a banana into the bowl and jumped out of the window, just as Cat came back with the sugar!

Cat poured in the sugar and stirred the mixture with a big wooden spoon. Then he emptied the bowl into a baking pan and popped it into the oven.

The following day Cat invited his
friends in for a snack.

"It's a chocolate cake today,"
said Cat. "I hope you'll like it!"

Cat cut the cake into seven slices.

"It looks good," said Bear.

"It smells good," said Tiger.

And all of them agreed it tasted . . .

...awful!

Except Goat, who giggled and said, "All the more for me!"

Because, as you know, goats will eat almost *anything*.

Cat still bakes a cake every week,
and they all turn out perfectly.
Probably because he always makes sure
the kitchen window is shut tight!